Hangin' with the Lil' Bratz

The scanning, uploading, and distribution of this book via the Internet or via any other means without the permission of the publisher is illegal and punishable by law. Please purchase only authorized electronic editions, and do not participate in or encourage electronic piracy of copyrighted materials. Your support of the author's rights is appreciated.

www.bratzpack.com
TM & © 2004 MGA Entertainment, Inc. Lil' Bratz and all related logos, names and distinctive likenesses are the exclusive property of MGA Entertainment, Inc. All Rights Reserved.

Used under license by Penguin Young Readers Group.
Published in Great Britain by Ladybird Books Ltd 2004
80 Strand London WC2R 0RL
A Penguin Company

ISBN 1 8442 2521 6   10 9 8 7 6 5 4 3 2 1

I'm **TALIA**, but my friends call me "Superstar" because I love to be in the spotlight. I really like to sing, but I love cool clothes and my fabulous friends even more!

My Diary

Today was super cool! My friends and I went to the mall to go shopping for new clothes. When we got to my absolute fave store, I found a cute sparkly purple top and embroidered jeans to match.

Then I remembered that Ailani's birthday is next week, so I slipped away and picked out a funky rainbow headband I just know she's going to love! I can't wait to give it to her at next weekend's birthday bash!

Talia

True blue friend

Always in the spotlight

Loves to shop

Into sparkles

A superstar!

I'm **NAZALIA**, but my friends call me "Butterfly" because I'm always fluttering from one thing to the next! I love dancing and shopping with my amazing friends!

My Diary

Today was totally great! On my way home from school, I walked past Talia's house and stopped in to say hi. We listened to her new CD and we spent the whole afternoon dancing to the funky beats of our favorite band.

Then she showed me the amazing headband she bought Ailani for her birthday, and I realized I completely forgot to get her something! It's time for this crafty girl to break out the beads and wire and design a funky necklace for my fabulous friend!

Nazalia

Lil' Bratz™

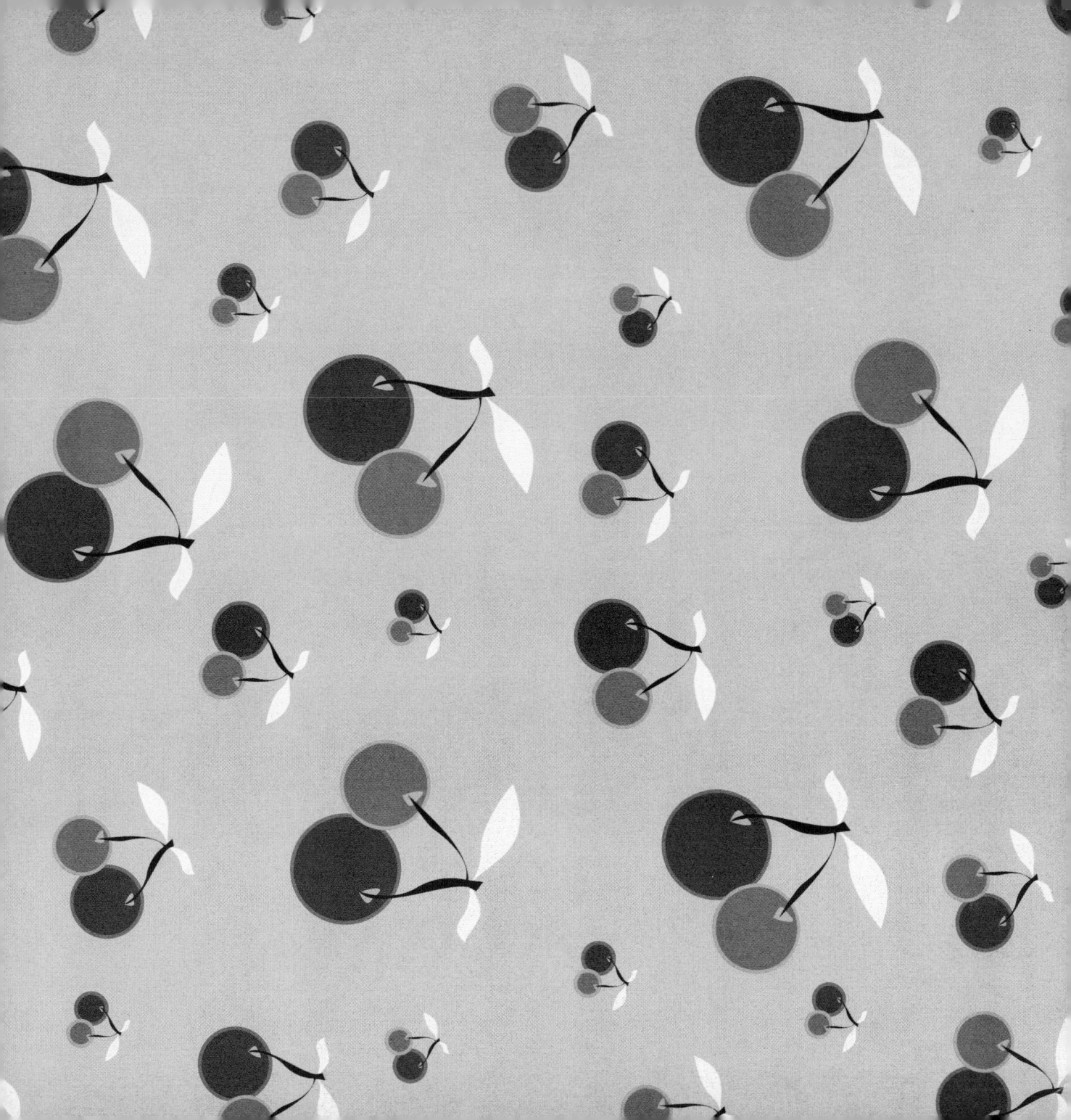

Lil Bratz

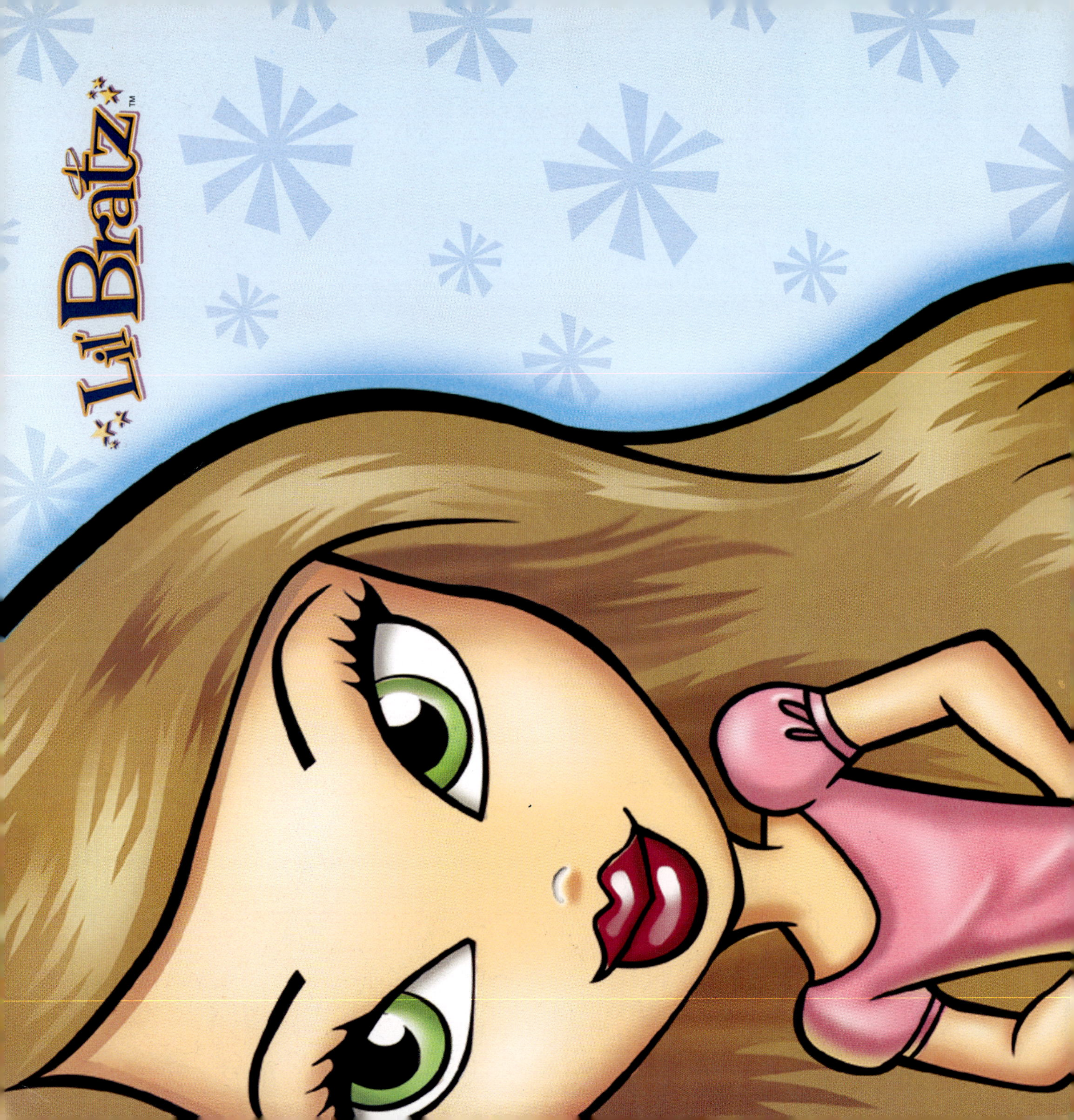
Lil' Bratz

Lil' Bratz

Zada™

Talia™

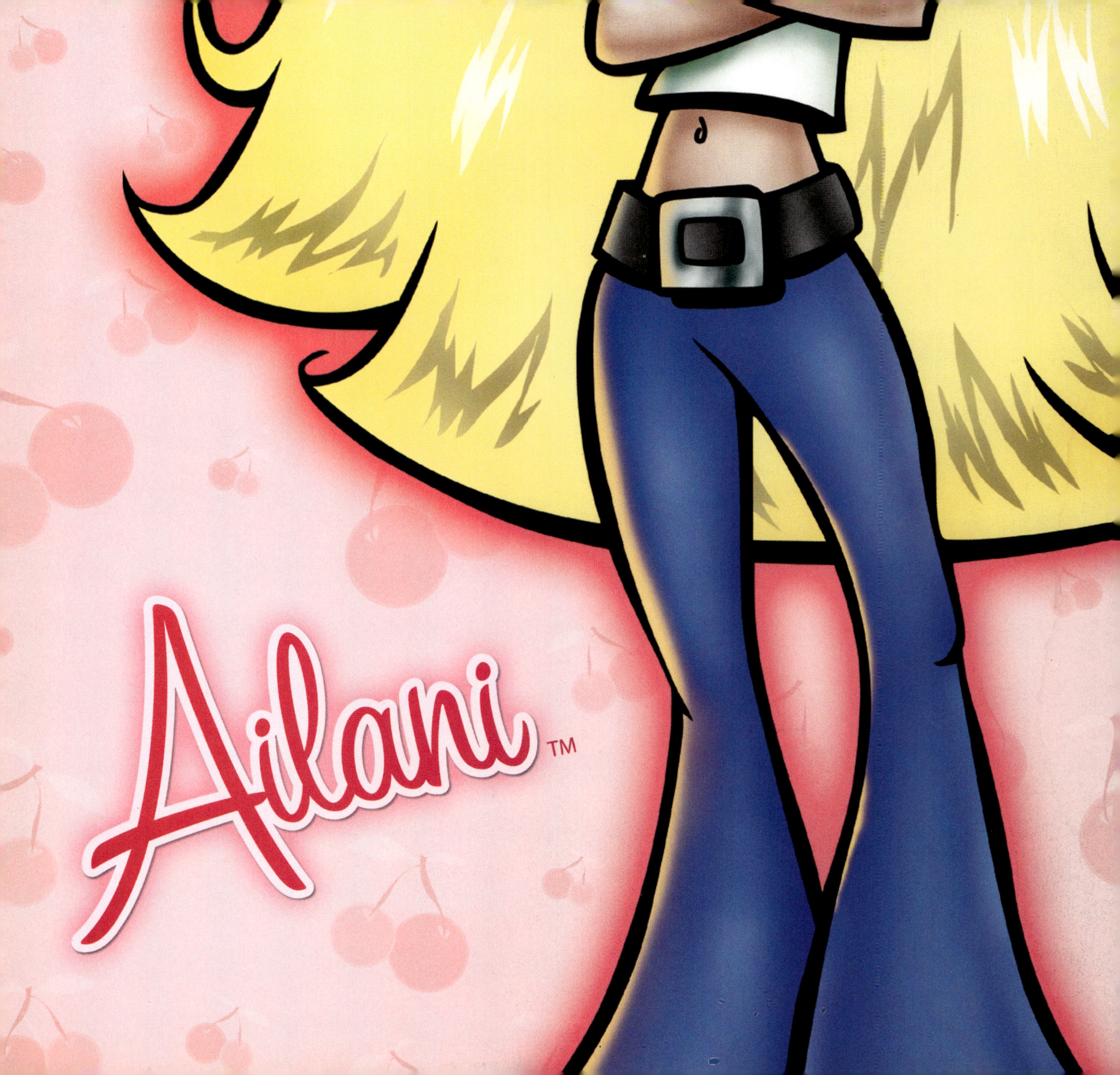
Ailani™

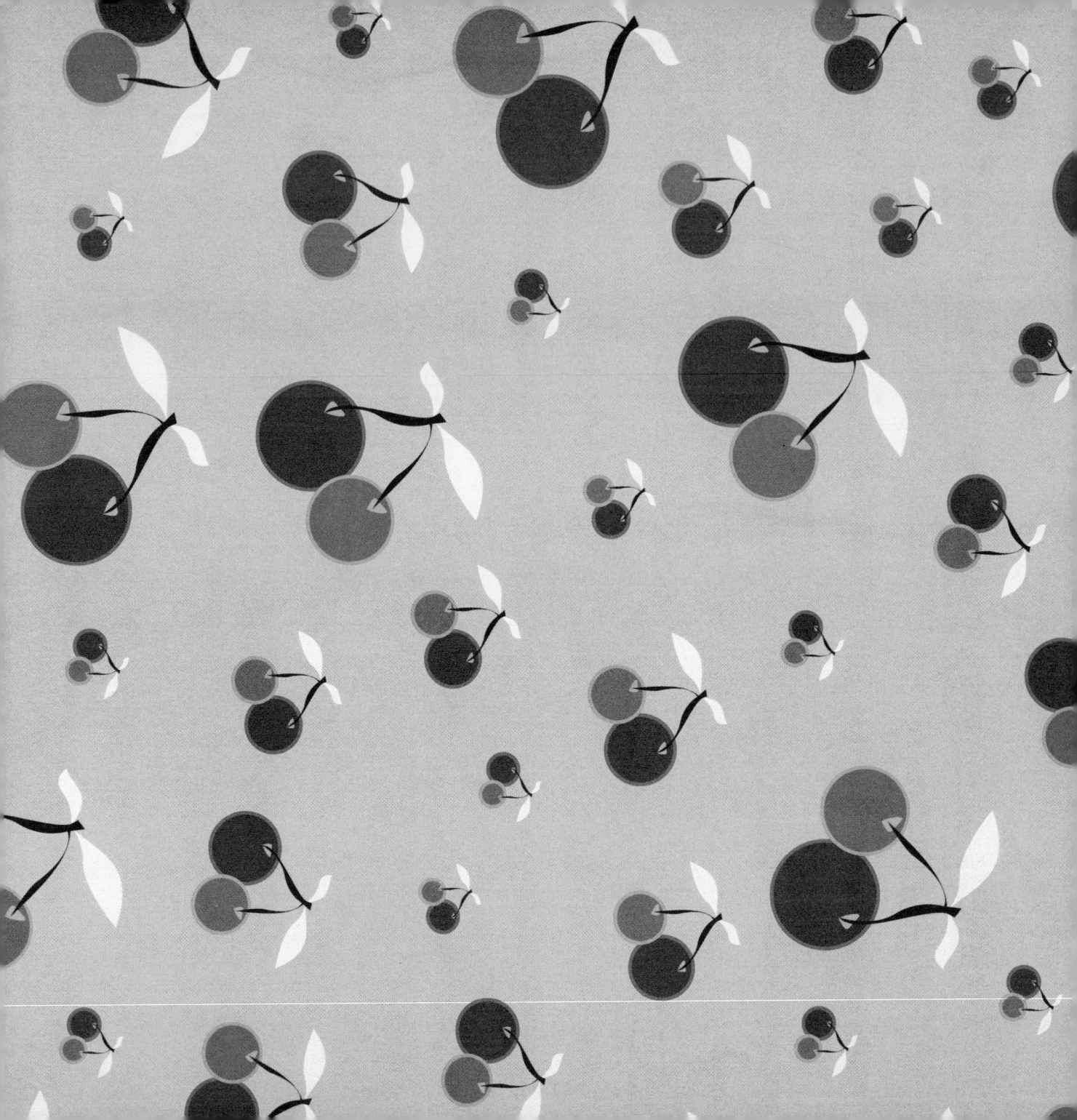

Nazalia™

Nice to everyone

Always in style

Zips around

A thoughtful friend

Loves to dance

Is called "Butterfly"

An amazing artist!

I'm **Zada**, but my friends call me "Sweet Heart" because I'm really sweet. I love animals, and I also love sharing clothes and exchanging outfits with my best friends.

My Diary

Wow! What a day! It sounded like someone was crying outside of my bedroom window, and when I went to check it out, it turned out our neighbor's cat was stuck in a tree! I ran outside to help, and we were able to get her out without a problem.

Then I headed to the salon for a haircut. I really love it... I think it looks funkadelic! I'm super-psyched to show my friends. Can't wait for tomorrow... I always have a great day when I'm feeling good inside and out!

♥ Zada

Z illions of smiles to share

A real sweetie

D reams of traveling

A nimal lover

I'm **Ailani**, but my friends call me "Cherrie." I love parties. One of my favorite things to do is to get all dressed up for a day at the mall!

My Diary

It's my birthday next week! I'm so psyched, because I'm having a sleepover party with my three best friends—Talia, Zada, and Nazalia! It's going to be totally awesome! We'll give one another manicures and pedicures. I know Talia, Zada, and Nazalia will love trying out the funky new nail polishes I bought too!

Then we'll have time for a movie before we put on our stylin' pajamas and get some beauty sleep. I love spending fun time with my friends. Only five more days to go . . .

Ailani

A lways up for a party
I s a real leader
L oves sleepovers
A wesome listener
N othing gets her down
I s a great friend!

Hope you had fun hangin' with us! Now put up our fabulously funkadelic posters in your locker or room so we can hang with you too!